D0568811

THE ABOMINABLE SNOW TEACHER

LISA PASSEN

HENRY HOLT AND COMPANY · NEW YORK

Henry Holt and Company, LLC

Publishers since 1866

115 West 18th Street, New York, New York 10011

www.henryholt.com

Henry Holt is a registered trademark of Henry Holt and Company, LLC

Distributed in Canada by H. B. Fenn and Company Ltd.

Library of Congress Catalog Card Number: 2003022494

Full Library of Congress Cataloging-in-Publication Data available at http://catalog.loc.gov/

ISBN 0-8050-7379-5 / EAN 978-0-8050-7379-9 / First Edition—2004

Designed by Donna Mark

Printed in the United States of America on acid-free paper. ∞

1 3 5 7 9 10 8 6 4 2

The artist used watercolor on 300-pound hot-press Lanaquarelle paper
to create the illustrations for this book.

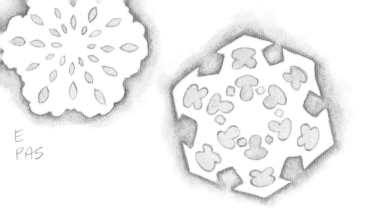

To Ma

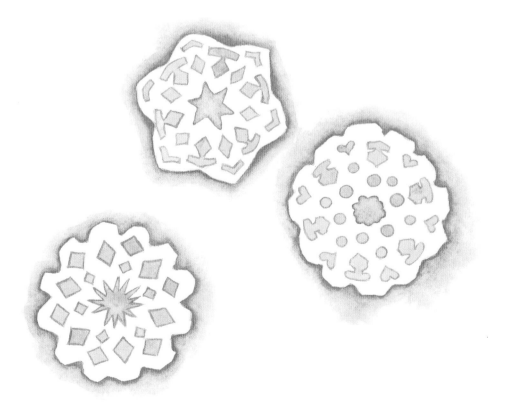

Miss Irma Birmbaum was
the toughest teacher in town.

But none of her students cared. School was cancelled for a snow day.

The children laughed and played in the snow and didn't think once about their schoolwork.

Miss Irma Birmbaum put on ski boots and headed out her front door.

"I must get to the school. My students need their textbooks and worksheets. I cannot let a day of education be wasted!"

Miss Birmbaum trekked through town unnoticed by the happy children at play.

"Oh, horrors!" exclaimed Miss Irma Birmbaum.
"The school is locked! My poor students. What will
they do today without their books?"

The children enjoyed a lively snowball toss.
Johnny O'Leary threw one a little too high. It hit
a telephone pole. Sparks erupted.

Mysterious lights headed north across the telephone wire, bounced across to East Lake School, and hit Miss Birmbaum!

Miss Irma Birmbaum jumped back.

She felt funny.

Her stockings started to itch.

She took off her glasses and rubbed her eyes.

Miss Irma Birmbaum put her glasses back on and
looked at her hands. They had fur. So did her face. She
had grown incredibly hairy. Miss Irma Birmbaum was
now an Abominable Snow Teacher!

Principal Renfield was out walking his dog, Cuddles.

"Miss Birmbaum!" exclaimed Principal Renfield.

"You're not looking yourself today."

Cuddles barked and growled at Miss Birmbaum.

He chased her.

His leash got tangled around the furry teacher. He took off down the middle of the street, dragging Miss Birmbaum behind him.

"No, Cuddles!" shouted Principal Renfield. "Bad dog!"

Rubi Flint was almost done making a snowman when Cuddles and Miss Birmbaum raced by. Rubi dropped her carrot in the snow and ran to warn the others.

"Miss Birmbaum is coming! Miss Birmbaum is coming!" she cried.

"Big deal," said Johnny. "She can't bother us. It's a snow day."

"You don't understand," said Rubi. "Miss Birmbaum is a . . . is a . . ."

"Look at Miss Birmbaum!" shouted Sheryl Shackmeyer.

"EEEKKKKKKK! An Abominable Snow Teacher!" screamed the children.

Miss Birmbaum and Cuddles crashed into a snowdrift.

Miss Birmbaum stood up and shook snow off her jacket.
She staggered toward her students. Everyone ran away.

"Where are you children going?" asked Miss Birmbaum.
"We must practice our multiplication!"

"Help! Help!" screamed Rubi.

"How do you spell *RESPECT*?" Miss Irma Birmbaum's
voice echoed through the snow-covered streets.

"Miss Birmbaum's gonna get us!" yelled Johnny.
"We gotta stop her!"

Johnny rolled a snowball down the steep hill.
It grew bigger and bigger and bigger.

The giant snowball smashed into the Abominable Snow Teacher, but it didn't stop her.

"What's the capital city of Alabama?" Miss Birmbaum asked her students.

"Oh, no!" said Sheryl.

Principal Renfield panted as he reached the children.
"Stay ca-calm, everyone. I'll pro-protect you!"
"What is 12 + 2?" questioned Miss Irma Birmbaum.
"Miss Birmbaum!" yelled the principal. "You are out
of control! It is a snow day. This is no time for testing!"

But Miss Birmbaum went on.

"How many legs does a spider have?"

At that very moment snow began to fall.

It got very windy.

The wind spun Miss Irma Birmbaum round and round. She grew dizzy.

"2+2 is 22!" she exclaimed. "*Dog* is spelled C-A-T!"

The mysterious lights returned. Miss Irma Birmbaum
felt funny again. Her stockings started to itch. She took
off her glasses and rubbed her eyes.

The snow stopped falling.

Miss Birmbaum put her glasses back on.

And then something *really* strange happened.

Miss Irma Birmbaum laughed and dove backward into the snow!

"Look at me!" exclaimed Miss Birmbaum.

Cuddles licked her whiskers.

"Is Miss Birmbaum feeling okay?" Johnny asked
Principal Renfield. The principal just smiled.

Miss Birmbaum played in the snow for the rest of the afternoon. Then the sun went down and the children were called home. Cuddles and Principal Renfield left too.

Miss Irma Birmbaum returned to her house alone. She warmed up in a hot bubble bath.

"What a peculiar feeling I had today," she thought to herself. "I think it's called . . . FUN."

Silvery-pink hairs began to wash off Miss Birmbaum.

The next day at school, Miss Irma Birmbaum
was her old self again . . .

. . . well, almost.